VAMPIRE PETER

BEN MANLEY   HANNAH PECK

Andersen Press

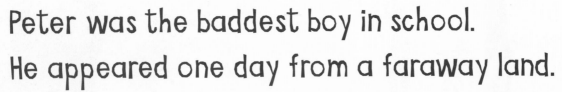

Peter was the baddest boy in school.
He appeared one day from a faraway land.

And everything he did was strange.

He wore strange clothes.
He ate strange food.

He liked strange things.

And his family were even stranger.

† "Shall I destroy her, your Majesty?"
†† "No, Orlok. She's my friend."

Because Peter didn't fit in,
he didn't have many friends.
And he was always in trouble...

For showing off in gym class.

For scaring Mr Renfield.

For fighting in the playground.

For not telling the truth.

But it wasn't Peter.

It was me.

I opened the cage to stroke Jonathan.
And I forgot to close the door.

I was worried I'd get into trouble, so I said nothing.
And I let Peter take the blame.

After all, he was the
baddest boy in school.

But, when I thought about it,
I knew that wasn't true.

He made me laugh
when I was sad.

He played with me when I
was on my own.

He stood up for me when I was in trouble.

Peter was my friend.

I did a terrible thing.
And I thought I would never be forgiven.
But I was wrong.

Everyone said Peter was the
baddest boy in school.
And maybe sometimes he is.

But most of the time,

Peter is the best.